To France and Pierre
M. B.

To Ghislaine and Mathieu
M. H. H.

First English-language edition 1990

English-language translation by Aliyah Morgenstern

Library of Congress Catalog Card Number 89-84466

10 9 8 7 6 5 4 3 2 1

First published in France in 1989 by
Editions Pastel, an imprint of l'école des loisirs

Published simultaneously in Canada
by Little, Brown & Company (Canada) Limited

Printed in Belgium

The Wedding of
Brown Bear and White Bear

by Martine Beck
Illustrated by Marie H. Henry

Little, Brown and Company
Boston Toronto London

Brown Bear lived in the mountains near the village of Hazelnutley. He never went out without his Tyrolean hat with the long red feather.

Brown Bear was an excellent fisherman. He was also an excellent cook.
He knew how to make a fire, using a few dried fir branches, to cook his fish.

Sometimes at night he felt a little bit sad without really knowing why.

One day, on his way to the village to go shopping, he stopped at a pond to watch the skaters.

A graceful white bear was merrily sliding on the glassy surface.

She would leap, twist, and turn, as her scarf fluttered around her like a cloud floating in the wind.

She was just so pretty!

Reluctantly, Brown Bear continued on his way to the market.
But he was smiling . . .

That evening, as he tried to read *The Daily Bear News*, his thoughts wandered.

The next day he went back to the pond.
The first thing he saw was White Bear's scarf. His heart started to beat faster.
She was just so graceful!
When she skated by, he caught a whiff of her sweet-smelling snowdrop and fir perfume.

That night, he dreamt that he was a wonderful skater dancing on the ice with the beautiful white bear in his arms.

The next morning the sun woke him up.
　　His dream had put him in such a good mood that he went right outside
to do his chores.

Then he washed up, combed his hair, and put on his very best clothes.

He walked briskly over to the skating pond, but White Bear wasn't there!
He walked around and around the lake.
He waited for a long time, a very long time. His heart was frozen.

The sky had turned gray and cloudy, and the fir trees cast a long shadow on the path.

Back home, nothing could warm him up as he climbed into bed.

The next day he kept himself as busy as possible until it was time to run back to the lake.

How wonderful it was to see the scarf floating in the air!
He rented a pair of skates and dashed onto the ice.
Thump! Crash! Flat on his nose!
Just as the beautiful white bear skated by!

There he was, furious and miserable, when he heard a sweet voice asking him, "Did you hurt yourself?"

He raised his head and saw White Bear's lovely smile.
"No, not at all!" he groaned.
She gave him her paw to help him up.
Her eyes were just so beautiful!

Big snowflakes were starting to fall.
"Would you like to have a cup of hot
chocolate with me?" he asked.
"That's a lovely idea," she said. "I'm
tired of skating."

Brown Bear brought her to a cabin in the village, where two lady bears made delicious blueberry pies.

White Bear's lips turned blue.

The next day they met under the branches of a big pine tree to go skiing.

Brown Bear zigzagged between the firs, proudly showing White Bear what a good skier he was.

Another time, they climbed to the top of the snow-covered peaks to admire the view. They spent more and more time together. In the village, whenever anyone saw the Tyrolean hat with the long red feather, they looked for the scarf trailing at its side.

One night the two bears saw a shooting star light up the sky.
"Quick! Make a wish!" she whispered to him.
"I wish we could always be together," he said.
And she smiled . . .

When he got home, Brown Bear wrote her a letter.

My dear beautiful White Bear,
Your eyes as bright as stars,
and your fur whiter than the moon,
have captured my heart.
Would you like to look at the moon and the stars
with me always and forever?

He slipped the letter into an envelope and entrusted it to his friend the owl.

White Bear read the letter and handed the owl her delicate scarf.
That's how Brown Bear would know she accepted.

All their friends came to the wedding. They watched Brown Bear tenderly place a crown of wild roses on White Bear's head. Then he gave her a big kiss.

Everybody clapped and the party began.
They formed a circle as the rhythm of the music echoed in the mountains.
Brown Bear and White Bear danced away until the last of the stars slipped out of the sky.